WANTED

DEVILS POINT WOLVES (MATING SEASON)

ELIZA GAYLE

GYPSY INK BOOKS

GET THE NEWS

Make sure you sign up for my newsletter for all the up-to-date book news, FREE books, and lots of behind the scenes goodies.

Join the exclusive list here: http://elizagayle.com/newsletter

PRO TIP: Make sure you add eliza@elizagayle.com to your contacts list to ensure the newsletter goes straight to your inbox.

ABOUT THE BOOK

by Eliza Gayle

Published by Gypsy Ink Books, © 2015 Eliza Gayle

eliza@elizagayle.com
http://ElizaGayle.com
Eliza on Tiktok - @elizagayleauthor
Eliza on Facebook - AuthorElizaGayle
Eliza on Instagram - ElizaGayleAuthor

Sign up for Eliza's Newsletter - elizagayle.com/news

Book Description:

Allison Fox is on the hunt again. Except this time the werewolf she's been assigned to track is her brother. The search has led to the island of Devils Point and it doesn't take her long to figure out she's hit the mother lode—of werewolves. But when she meets Diego, her world turns upside down.

As mating season comes to a close, Diego is thrown into chaos when he's given the task of interrogating the female hunter who would like nothing more than to kill him. His track record with women sucks and this one is no better. Especially when his wolf stands up and claims her as his mate.

Allison Fox twisted in the sand, putting the handcuffs holding her wrists underneath her and came face to face with a devil.

A dark eyed, dark haired gorgeous devil at that whose every tall, muscled inch towered over her. Despite the scowl and the danger emanating from him, the man underneath intrigued her.

She recognized her captor as Diego, one of the brothers who owned Club Diablo. A strip club that sat at the entrance to Devils Point, the island these men called home.

Except these were no ordinary men. They were dangerous werewolves who threatened humanity with their very existence. Although they were nothing like the wolves she'd encountered in the past.

These were clean, well dressed and rather articulate. It hadn't been easy identifying them as shifters at first.

Except this was their mating season, the one time a year they lost control when it came to their need to mate. And with such single-minded focus distracting them, they tended to let their guards down.

"You got her, Diego? Or do you need our help getting her home?"

She turned to the voice to see Dante and Damien also staring down at her. Although they were shifting around as if antsy to get the hell out of there.

"Not much to it. Look at her. She's like a scrawny rat. I can easily handle her alone."

Scrawny rat. She took offense at his assessment of her but kept her mouth firmly shut. The less she engaged the better. Besides, her energy was better used to figure out her escape. She still had a mission to accomplish before she could go home.

"Good, we're headed back home to check on the others. But Chess and Branch will be around if you need some help."

Diego leaned down and grabbed her around the shoulder and hauled her to her feet. Effortlessly she noted. No small feat for her one hundred and seventy pounds. He might have compared her to a scrawny rat, but she was far from it. Thanks to her family genes she was stocky at best and overweight at worst. And no diet in the world seemed to change that.

"Let me go," she demanded, wrenching her arm free from his hold.

"No," Diego said.

"Have fun little brother. Don't forget to call if you need some help handling her." Both men disappeared into the woods amidst guffaws and snickers. Whatever was so funny she didn't understand.

"You can't hold me like this. I have rights."

He glared at her, the intensity in his eyes allowing some of her fear to get the better of her.

"You gave up your rights when you tried to shoot my brother." Diego wrapped his hand around her arm just above the elbow and steered her in the direction his brothers had gone.

Handcuffed and having been divested of all of her primary weapons, even the small hunting knife she kept in her boot, she had no choice but to go with him and hope as time went on she'd discover a way to break free and then make these wolves pay.

"Why did you try to shoot him?"

"He's a werewolf. Why wouldn't I?"

"That's a shitty answer."

Allison shrugged. "It's the truth."

He stopped and hauled her close. So close there was barely a breath between them and she immediately felt his body heat. And his scent. It didn't take supernatural anything to identify the woodsy outdoors mixed with the spice of his soap. It was a heady mix.

More than that. He was somehow screwing with her brain. She couldn't exactly focus on anything but him and how good he felt this close to her.

She planted her hands on this chest and tried to push away. "Whatever you're doing to me stop it. I don't do wolves and getting inside my head won't change that."

"You don't do wolves." He repeated her statement very slowly and with a low growl behind it. "And how exactly am I getting in your head? I haven't even begun to interrogate you."

"I don't know," she said, shaking her head. "I just know something's not right and you must be the cause of it."

He rolled his eyes and continued his trek, pulling her along with him. "You're nuts and I don't mean that in some cute way like you humans think. I was at a party, minding my own business. I sure as hell didn't need this shit tonight. I mean look at that moon. Do you even know what that means?"

"Your mating season is coming to an end?" She glanced up at the near full moon shining unbelievably bright in the sky and took a scientific guess based on what she'd been taught.

"How do you know that?" he demanded.

"Just lucky I guess."

He shook his head and she heard that low growl again. "This is not how you want to play it with me tonight. I'm already on edge. Having to deal with you isn't helping."

"This isn't exactly a party for me either. These handcuffs are digging into my wrists and I'm being dragged deep into the woods by a beast. Last time I checked that doesn't bode well for me."

"This isn't a horror movie. I have no cabin in these woods where I take nosy, dangerous humans like you and slaughter them."

She stumbled before righting herself. "But you do have a home out here?" she asked.

"Yeah, the one you shot up earlier. I live there with my brother."

Interesting. "Sounds like you and your brother are close."

"We are. Which is why I'm a little put out that you tried to kill him tonight."

"If I had tried to kill him he would be dead. I haven't missed a shot like that since I was twelve and learning to shoot."

Diego whipped around and she crashed into him face first considering the top of her head barely came to his shoulders. This was no ordinary crash though. Never in her life had she landed on such a finely sculpted wall of muscle. The few guys she'd let get this close were not built like this. Athletic yes, extraordinary specimens, no.

"Would you please stop doing that?"

His chest rumbled under her cheek. "What's wrong, little girl, are you afraid of the big bad wolf?"

"Hardly. I just have no need for you in my personal space."

He shifted closer and she could have sworn for a fleeting second he was hard. And this time she wasn't referring to his chest or abs. Allison sucked in a breath.

For a few long seconds neither of them spoke and all she heard was the roaring of her pulse in her ears. Or maybe it was the erratic and wild tempo of her heartbeat. No, she wasn't exactly afraid of the wolf, but this wasn't like her previous encounters and she couldn't explain why being so close to this one made her heart beat double time or her body ache.

"Get in," he ordered.

She blinked and looked up at him, not entirely sure she heard him correctly.

"What do you—" He nodded his head to the right and she turned to see he was directing her toward a dark, open topped jeep with big tires on it that were great for mudding.

"Uhm, no thanks," she said. "I don't take rides from strangers."

He sighed and wrapped his hands around her waist and lifted her where he wanted her. A pulsing shock of electricity coursed through her at his touch. For a second all she could focus on was that tiny contact and by the time enough of her wits returned to focus, he was already walking around the vehicle and getting in.

"I demand you let me go." She was beginning to panic. Between the weird unexplained reactions to his touch and the fear of being held captive in some wolf lair, she had to exert some control into the situation.

"I wanted a carefree party and maybe a dick sucking tonight. I guess neither of us is going to get what we want."

Her brain tripped and melted. His vulgar reference to oral sex should have pissed her off or at the very least grossed her out at the image that painted in her head. So why had the ache in her chest suddenly traveled south. Not once had anyone in her family mentioned that wolves had special pheromones that could ensnare her. But why else was she having such a visceral reaction to a man like him? He was supposed to be disgusting and bloodthirsty and a danger to human society.

She wasn't supposed to want to screw his brains out within five minutes of meeting him.

Obviously unaffected or unaware of what was going on with her, he started the engine and took off.

Diego pushed the pedal hard and drove them across the island at top speed despite the twists and turns and bumpy road conditions. He didn't care. Maybe white knuckling the steering wheel and forcing his concentration on the road would get his mind off the woman sitting in the passenger seat, taunting him.

Although with his head filled with her scent and the feel of her breasts pushed against his chest imprinted in his mind for all eternity he doubted anything would work right now. One more night was all he'd needed. One more long night of mating season and he would have been home free for another year. And instead the worst possible choice sat next to him while all he could think about was getting inside her.

He hated this shit. Mating season was supposed to be some great thing. A way for wolves to ensure their lines by hooking up and procreating. All he saw it as was a weakness and he had no time or inclination for weakness.

The fact both his brothers had accepted their mates this season didn't phase him. Damien had been circling Faith from a distance for a while despite his protests and Dante could only survive so long in denial.

He, on the other hand, had discovered no mate and was okay with that. He had a good and simple life here on the island and hadn't reached the point he wanted to share that with anyone. Tonight changed everything.

Based on her scent and his reaction, he had a feeling he was going to get more than he bargained for. A woman who could be his mate but who also wanted to kill him and all his kind. A hunter.

Just fucking lovely.

"So how about we start somewhere easy," he asked.

She ignored him, staring out the windshield.

"How did you end up on Devils Point? We don't exactly advertise our location to your kind."

The seconds ticked by so long, he didn't think she would answer when she finally spoke.

"I came here looking for someone."

His body locked up. This didn't sound good. "Who? Your boyfriend? Husband?"

"That's none of your business."

"You took several shots at my pack. Almost killed my brother. Everything about you is now my business. Including your fate."

Her head whipped to the side and he met her gaze.

"My fate is you need to let me go," she said, a steel thread laced in her tone. "And I already told you that I wasn't trying to kill your brother."

Despite his admiration for her strength, he shook his head. "Not going to happen. All I know is that you're one of them hunters who think we're evil and they want nothing more than to eradicate us all. Since we'd like to keep on living in peace, and unless you convince me otherwise, you aren't going anywhere."

"You could escort me off island. I'd be happy to go."

"So you can come back with reinforcements? No thanks."

She didn't respond and he kept his eyes on the road. He was supposed to take her to the basement for questioning and safekeeping, but the idea of being locked in a tiny confined space with her did not sound like a good idea. Her scent was already making him weird.

He could keep his baser urges under lockdown, but that didn't mean he had to make it unnecessarily hard. No, for now the basement was out of the question.

Instead he turned towards the small campground/park at the south end of the island. There weren't a lot of tourists on the island at the moment so they'd be alone in a wide open space with plenty of fresh air.

Perfect.

They rode in silence for the rest of the ride, but he noticed her searching the horizon when he approached the beach.

"Uhm…Where are you taking me?"

"Somewhere private," he answered.

He pulled into the end of the parking lot and circumvented the conventional parking spaces and went straight for the beach. For his sanity, he wanted to be near the water. While his wolf craved the forested areas of the island, his human half sought the serenity from the waters surrounding them.

With the chaos of the last of mating season still weighing down on him, he needed to get free of the confines of his truck cab—and quick.

He pulled up to one of the tiny enclosed pavilions normally reserved for birthday parties or the occasional wedding and turned off the engine. He opened the door and hopped out of the cab, rounding the front to the passenger door.

"I'm not going anywhere with you," she said out the partially opened window.

He smirked. As if she had a choice. He yanked the door open and grabbed the woman around the waist. He easily lifted her out of the seat and tossed her over his shoulder.

"Hey!"

He ignored her protests and wrapped his arm around her legs so she couldn't break free if she tried.

"You can't do this. I have rights."

"Then you should have thought about that before you came here and attacked. You were unprovoked."

"You're an animal," she cried. "We have no choice but to take matters into our own hands. Isn't that the law of the jungle?"

"Look, lady, I don't know shit about the jungle. Look around you. You see any jungles here? This is civilization not some safari out in the wilds."

Diego slammed the door to the pavilion open and dropped the woman into the nearest chair. It had been a long time since he'd had to listen to this kind of crap.

"You're nuts," he said. "We're law abiding citizens. Whatever you think we do is all in your imagination."

Her eyes bulged and her face turned red. "You do hurt people. I've seen it." Her voice grew louder. "I've seen first hand what it looks like when your kind gets angry. I've seen throats ripped out, body limbs mangled and women gutted from hip to breast. It's vicious and disgusting. Pure evil."

Diego watched her body shake as she yelled at him. The horror she described played across her face, heartbreak and anguish etched into her eyes with every word she spoke.

He squatted down in front of her chair bringing them eye to eye. He was supposed to loathe her for every hate filled word that spewed from her mouth. But it wasn't hate he sensed—it was pain.

"I don't hurt people unless they hurt me first. Neither does my pack. In fact, we avoid confrontation as much as possible." He took a deep breath and continued, hoping his voice remained steady. "But there is evil in this world. I've seen it too. I lost part of my family to it. I've even spent a fair amount of my time hating humans as much as you've hated shifters. Until I was forced to learn that blaming an entire species based on the reactions of a few is weakness. And weakness is unacceptable."

He paused long enough to see the moisture shining in her eyes and he waited. But her tears never fell. An immense sensation washed through him. Pride. He couldn't believe how happy he was when she didn't resort to water works to sway him.

"I would hate anyone who preyed on the innocent, not just shifters," she whispered.

"The people who come after us are far from innocent. They're instigators looking for trouble. Or an excuse to justify their weakness. Your group is weak like that too. It's why you'll never win."

Her eyes narrowed and her face turned hard. "You don't know me or my group. You think you do, but you don't. You assume. Talk about a weakness…"

Diego bristled, the wolf growling in his head. He tamped down on the anger building inside him. Anger, lust, the moon. It was all too much and getting more difficult by the second. He stood and walked to the open window that overlooked the ocean. The rhythmic lapping of the water against the shoreline capturing his attention. Over and over he listened to each repeating cycle. It wasn't just mesmerizing it was comforting to count on the water to always be there, day after day, greeting him with the same patterns. There was never any need to question its intentions or debate whether it would still be there the next day. It always was.

The ocean was and always would be his most faithful companion.

Without turning back to the woman pulling at him, he spoke again. "Then enlighten me. Tell me what I've assumed about you that isn't correct."

She laughed. A harsh but lyrical sound that scraped against his resistance. He almost turned to her, but caught himself before he did, willing his body to behave.

"It's not my job to enlighten anyone. Enlighten yourself."

Unable to resist again, he turned and watched her in the moonlight. Her golden hair shone silvery like the stars in the night sky, pale skin practically glowing, and the fragile slope of her neck made his teeth ache with need. He took a step forward completely transfixed. Far more than his need to bite her, his body drew taut. The heat rushing through his blood was threatening to consume him.

What would she taste like?

When he took another step closer, her eyes widened but she wisely kept her mouth shut. He wanted her and it was fast becoming his single-minded focus. With the mating bond he could easily turn her and she'd never again be a threat. Her group would try to hunt her, but never find a trace of the woman they once knew. He'd make sure of it.

Diego would do whatever it took to protect his mate.

Thinking the word made his head snap back and some of the fog clouding his mind cleared.

He couldn't do this. This took keeping your enemies close to a whole new dangerous level. And of course turning her against her will was completely out of the question. Not to mention risky. Faith had recently went through that thanks to their damned rogue running loose and it could have killed her. Fortunately, the bond between her and Damien proved true. As for this one...

"You might want to rethink that stance. It's my job to discover every secret you have and I'm authorized to take whatever means are necessary to ensure my pack's safety."

"Screw you," she spat. "You want to torture me? Go right ahead."

He took her words as every bit of a challenge as they were meant and he closed the distance between them. Towering over her he waited for her to attack him. There wasn't any doubt in his mind she'd fight him hard, but his superior strength meant she'd lose and lose bad.

"That's what you want me to do? Torture the information out of you? Are you sure about that?"

The pain from before flashed across her face a moment before it was replaced with anger and she lowered her voice to a whisper. "You wouldn't be the first."

His body locked tight as the meaning of her words sank in. The wolf inside snarled in his head a moment before a rush of possessiveness washed over him. He saw red as he imagined her lush body used by another, while morphing into a vision of pure white-hot rage.

"Explain," he growled, not caring that the word barely sounded human.

"I don't have to—"

"Explain now," he ordered putting more rage in his voice this time.

Her eyes widened letting him know that she got the message loud and clear.

"It was a long time ago. A shifter in Seattle captured me. A mean son of a bitch who liked to play with his prey."

The haze of fury clouding Dante's mind thickened. "What did he do to you?"

She shook her head. "It doesn't matter. He's dead now."

"You killed him?" he asked.

She nodded.

"What did he do to you?" He couldn't let it go.

"Roughed me up a little."

"What else?" He could tell she was holding back.

She turned her head away and refused to look him in the eye. "It really doesn't matter anymore. It's ancient history."

"It matters to me," he whispered.

When she didn't respond or turn to look at him, he dipped his head close and breathed in her scent. The fact he was so close didn't seem so dangerous anymore. Or he didn't care. A mate no matter whether she is claimed or not deserved to be treasured.

"If you bite me, I WILL kill you," she said, her words an icy threat he didn't doubt she'd find a way to follow through on.

He pressed his nose to her neck and nuzzled. "I don't have to bite you against your will. Soon you will want it."

"Pffft. Don't count on that. Despite what you might think, Romeo, you are not irresistible."

"I'm not Romeo, I'm Diego." He pressed his lips to her fevered skin with a feather light touch. Her resulting shiver made him smile. Oh yes, a mate, potential or otherwise, would not resist him for long.

She jerked her body to the side and away from his mouth. "Back off, Romeo. That kind of seduction might work on those simpering women in your club, but it sure as hell doesn't work on me."

Diego pulled back, allowing his little spitfire some space for now. "It's not seduction you have to worry about, sweetheart. It's chemistry."

THREE

Allison's body froze on the whispered words of the wolf. What the hell was that supposed to mean. Chemistry? It had to be some trick he wanted her to fall for and she wasn't going to allow it.

"Rules of engagement in any warfare type of situation don't include sexual activities. So you might want to get that little nugget right out of your head."

Instead of the backlash of anger she expected, Romeo laughed. A deep hearty sound that crawled down her skin and landed smack dab between her legs.

Her body was clearly losing its mind. She refused to believe it was acting on the wishes of her brain and instead chose to believe it acted on a completely separate capacity that she had no control over. Why else would it respond to the man holding her captive?

"What makes you think I care about any rules of engagement?" he asked.

She met his gaze and stared. There was something about him that she couldn't quite put her fingers on. Honor maybe? Not exactly. He might think he was honorable but it wasn't the whole picture. It was true she'd engaged first and he had certain rights when it came to her capture, but there was definitely something more behind those brown eyes that looked dreamier than the melted chocolate she liked to dip her strawberries in.

"You say I shouldn't judge a species based on a bad few. If that's truly the case and your pack is not like the others then I would think you would care about rules of engagement. Are you retracting what you said before?"

It was a dare and a gamble at that. But the vibe she got from this shifter was completely different than her previous experiences.

It didn't come soaked in a cloak of human hatred. Instead, he seemed interested in her in a way that said, "you're not really my enemy" almost as much as it said, "I want you."

Although the second part could be her imagination. She didn't have a lot of experience when it came to the sexual interactions between men and women and she could have easily misread his intentions.

"Why don't you unfasten my hands and we'll see if we can come to some sort of truce?" she suggested.

"A truce huh? Maybe I don't need a truce."

"Then what do you need?" She had a feeling it was a loaded question on her part, but screw it. There was something different about this situation and she fully intended to explore it, right up to the point she got free.

He leaned into her again, putting his lips directly against her ear. "Right now I only need one thing and I'll give you want you want."

Her heart hammered in her throat as she considered the myriad of possibilities of what he wanted. This situation could easily spiral out of her control if she didn't tread carefully.

"What do you want, Romeo?" she asked, not caring if he didn't like her use of a nickname. She had a feeling it suited him. No man looked as delicious as he did without earning a certain reputation with the ladies. Men like him inspired women to fall at his feet and give him the world. And apparently she was included in that list because she had half a mind to give him anything he asked for.

His breath brushed her ear as she waited for him to tell her what he wanted. The short whiskers of his neatly trimmed beard tickled her when they rubbed against her. Or maybe it was she who was swaying toward him. It was impossible to think straight with him in her personal space, invading her with his decadence.

Maybe it was a good thing her hands were tied otherwise she might be tempted to sink them into his hair and pull him forward until his lips touched her again.

"Tell me your name, beautiful. That's all I need for now."

Allison jerked at the soft-spoken request. His earlier hints of control and demand all but disappeared. Her head spun.

He only wanted her name?

Her name...

What did it matter? She was a nobody. In the hierarchy of their organization she didn't even register. She couldn't be traded for anything of value because no one would care if she disappeared tomorrow. Yet, somehow giving it up to him felt powerful.

"Allison Fox," she whispered, so quiet he shouldn't have heard her.

But he did.

"Such a beautiful name for a beautiful woman. Welcome to Devils Point, Allison." The reverence in his voice stunned her. She almost melted on the spot.

She also didn't understand why he kept calling her beautiful. Maybe on a good day people would describe her as cute, but at the moment she was a big sweaty, dirty mess who smelled every bit as bad as she looked. But he called her beautiful.

She smiled, turning away from him and melted more than a little in her chair.

He on the other hand, moved behind her and fulfilled his promise. He untied her hands and even rubbed away some of the stiffness of her joints and arms from holding them behind her back for so long.

Sitting back against the chair she brought her hands in front and finished rubbing them down. "So what now? You letting me go?"

"Not quite. You're going to have to be my guest a bit longer. At least until I'm satisfied with your reasons for being here and what you plan to do next. I can't have a hunter running free on the island."

She contemplated what to tell him. Obviously she'd have to share something or he was going to continue wasting her time. "I'm searching for a wolf, but I doubt he's one of yours. Although someone here must be harboring him since I briefly spotted him here a couple of weeks back and nothing since."

She could tell by the swing of his head and the slight narrowing of his eyes that he knew exactly what wolf she referred to.

"That was you out by the bridge, wasn't it?" he asked. "The gunshot that scared the wolf away from Faith."

"Whose Faith?" She deflected his question with a question. She'd need more details before she gave him any more information.

"Pretty blonde, green mini cooper. Wolf bit her wrist a couple of weeks back. Mysterious gunshot scared him off before he could do worse."

"Girl okay?" The idea of her brother turning wolf and killing innocents churned in her stomach. Almost as much as the idea of what she'd have to do to him if she found out he was indeed taking life or making other wolves.

"She's fine, thanks to the mate bond she shares with my brother. Easily could have went south if not for that."

"Mate bond?"

He nodded. "Normally I wouldn't tell you more, but in this case, knowing how dangerous a wolf bite can be, I think I have to make an exception. A mate bond is what happens between a shifter and the person he's in love with. Or in the case of fated mates, the special person who's been selected by nature. Those bonds are apparently the shit and can be quite rare."

Allison pushed her hands through her hair and scrunched up her face as she let some of what he said sink in. "A fated mate? Like an arranged marriage?"

He nodded. "Something like that. Except the only person or thing making the arrangement is mother nature herself."

"I don't think I like that. Why would someone want to get marr—I mean bonded to someone they didn't love?"

"Or maybe not even know," he finished for her.

This had nothing to do with finding her brother and yet she was fascinated all the same.

"Funny thing is..." Diego continued. "I've never heard of a fated mate who didn't love their mate. My brother and Faith are out of their minds over each other. Granted, they've kind of known each other for a while and wasted a lot of time circling the truth. That wolf bite was a turning point for them, allowing them both to let down their guards. Now they can't keep away from each other for ten minutes. It's kind of nauseating."

Allison half laughed and half snickered. Diego's obvious distaste for this mating bond seemed half hearted.

"What about you then? Do you have a fated mate?"

He didn't utter a word, but he didn't have to. His body locked up and his stare in her direction grew intense before he turned away from her and looked out the window and toward the ocean. She had a feeling there was a hell of a story behind that reaction.

"Maybe we should talk about you and the reason you are hunting this one wolf in particular. Did he do something to you?"

With his back to her she couldn't make out his body language as well, but his question was now tinged with something sad. Or maybe dark. She really wanted to know more about this mate bond thing and in particular how it affected the man standing in front of her. What exactly was his story?

Captor or not, she was intrigued.

And drawn...

FOUR

Diego needed out. He needed to call in one of his brothers and ask them to take care of this situation. Except Faith was still struggling with her transition and needed to be kept under guard and Damien's wolf couldn't stand to let unmated wolves near her right now.

As for Dante, he was probably in the middle of some knock down drag out marathon sex session with Rebel that Diego had no intention of wading into. Especially not if he wanted to keep on breathing. He understood the possessive streak, because they all carried it.

He could probably ask Creed, one of the pack who often handled security, to take over with little grief. That man had a way with the ladies that no one saw coming. In fact, one look at him and most of them started throwing their panties. Allison wouldn't know what hit her until after Creed got and gave what he needed and walked out the door. Diego's wolf growled.

And there lie the real problem.

Turning her over to an unmated male was out of the question. His wolf sat too close to the surface on this one and if he took one step away from his potential mate, his own wolf would eat him alive.

Taking one last deep breath of ocean air, he turned back to her. "You haven't answered my question," he said.

"Does it really matter? He's not part of your pack so why worry about him?"

Diego crossed his arms over his chest and frowned. "Don't get me wrong. I love my pack and will protect them to my dying breath. But pack is not all I am. I'm also human. That rogue hurt my brother's mate, has been stalking another one of our women and I want to know why. I'm not going to let this go or you until I'm satisfied, so you might as well tell me."

The way her body vibrated as she sat in the chair made him wonder whether she'd run or attack first. He could see the debate going on behind her eyes. For a human she had fairly strong instincts and hers were telling her to get rid of the threat.

"Don't do it." He tried to swallow the accompanying growl and failed.

Her head swung up. "Don't do what?"

"Whatever it is your planning in that pretty little head of yours. I'd rather not have to chase you." Which was a big, juicy lie. He did want to chase her. So bad he could almost taste the spoils of his success.

Unable to resist the compulsion to be close to her, he took several steps forward again. "Do you understand what it does to a wolf when something he wants runs from him?"

She shook her head, wisely keeping her mouth shut.

"It makes you irresistible prey that he must have. Not later, not eventually, right that second. Everything else goes away. It's the instinct that makes a new wolf especially dangerous."

"You're not a new wolf."

"No, I'm not. But it is the last night of mating season and I'm hungry. Hungrier than I've ever been in my life." That was not a lie. "While the wolf is under control for the moment, the second you jump from that chair he's going to get what he wants. Do you understand what I mean?"

She swallowed hard, drawing his gaze to her slender throat. He zeroed in on the pulse beating there that drew him like a moth to a flame.

"You want to have sex with me," she said, squirming a little in her seat, her chest rising and falling in rapid succession with each breathless word.

"That's one way to put it."

She shook her head, working her way into a denial.

"Do you understand now why you can't run?"

She nodded.

"Although I am still going to fuck you, beautiful. Only not until you say pretty please."

Her eyes widened and she drew her bottom lip between her teeth. She might deny it if he asked, but it wasn't fear rushing through her at the moment. It was the unmistakable spicy scent of arousal.

Diego knew he'd crossed the line in this supposed interrogation. Instead of getting any useful information his pack could use against her kind or to find their rogue, he'd compromised the situation with selfish desires. And there wasn't a damn moment of it he regretted.

This pretty little human named Allison with her compact, curvy body had fallen into his lap by way of gunfire and one way or another he would find a way to keep her.

But first, they needed to get through the immediate problem.

"I take it you're not going to run?"

"No," she said on a shaky breath.

He reached forward and stroked his fingers down her cheek. "That's too bad. It would have been fun."

Diego dropped his hand and turned away. Her decision was for the best—for now. It didn't mean he wouldn't pursue her later. Or keep trying to find out more about her.

"So I guess we're back to my missing wolf," she said.

He stared out at the horizon and back, scanning the bay for something to focus on when his eye caught on something unusual. A faint light on Deadman's Island.

While Deadman's Island wasn't the official name for the tiny speck of land in their bay, its history as a Native American burial ground made the name stick with the locals. It was too small to sustain residents and it was illegal to stay out there beyond dusk.

He called on the wolf and forced the beginning of a partial change. Enough for his eyesight to sharpen to his wolf's.

The light in the distance grew brighter and he guessed it was an extremely small fire on the southeast corner that would be invisible to most of Devils Point. Had he not brought Allison out to the park he'd never have spotted it. Whoever was out there was doing their damndest to keep a low profile.

"I think I have an idea where we can start looking."

She jumped up from her chair. "Where?"

"Follow me."

Unconcerned with whether she would follow him (she would), Diego headed toward the boathouse where the rentals were stored. With the master key on his key ring, he unlocked the old building and entered ahead of Allison.

"Where are we? I can't see," she whispered behind him.

Because he didn't need any additional light to see the interior, he'd forgotten that little miss human didn't have super vision.

"Just stay there at the entrance and don't touch anything. I don't want to turn the lights on and give away our location to anyone who might see that we're this close."

"You think we're being watched?"

He grabbed one of the canoes and headed back to the door. "I'm almost certain, but I'm not taking any chances. That damned rogue has been elusive for too long. It's time to find him and end this tonight."

Allison sucked in a breath. "What's that supposed to mean?"

"Look, Allison. I know you're on some kind of mystery mission that you don't want to talk about. But if the rogue is feral we have a bigger problem than you or whoever your boss is wanting some sort of revenge."

The more he thought about what he'd learned so far, he leaned towards feral. Living alone too long without a pack could cause a wolf to go crazy. Although newbie could also explain the erratic behavior. Either way, he wasn't human and therefore they needed to be on guard.

"You think he's feral? What exactly does that... Uhm—why are you carrying a canoe?"

Out here in the moonlight she didn't need extra light to see what he was up to. "I saw a fire out on Deadman's Island and I'm going out there to check it out. Might be nothing, might be the elusive wolf. At least if we found him out there it would explain why he has continued to disappear on us."

"Where is this Deadman's Island?"

Diego pointed to the small circle of trees in the middle of the bay. "Right out there."

"And you think that's where the wolf is? How can you be sure?"

He shrugged. "I can't. But someone is out there and shouldn't be so I might as well check it out."

"Fine. I'm going with you."

He smiled. "Yeah, beautiful, you are. If I leave you here I'm sure you'll take off and then where will I be?"

In deep and pining alone, he thought to himself.

"I'm not leaving Devils Point until I find the wolf I'm looking for." She crossed her arms and cocked her hip.

"I'm still waiting on my answer on why this wolf is so important to you. There's got to be a catch in all this."

She raised her eyebrows. "Wait away."

Despite the severity of the situation he let the smile come instead of fighting it. Sassy and beautiful. He liked it.

"Why don't you grab a set of oars from the back of the door and we'll get this show on the road."

She peeked her head inside and grabbed two sets instead of one like he expected. Interesting.

"You always go this primitive? Isn't there a boat with a motor we can use somewhere? This seems so twentieth century."

He walked the canoe to the water and set it in. "Sure there are if you don't mind announcing your arrival from a mile away. Kind of takes away the element of surprise."

"Oh right. Super hearing, yes?"

He nodded. "Something like that."

Diego grabbed the end of the boat and held it in place. "Go ahead and hop in. I got this."

With little delay and smooth movements, Allison climbed into the boat and settled onto the front bench. He climbed in behind her and grabbed a set of the oars. She followed suit.

One minute they were captor and captive and next they were setting off on a little adventure as partners.

She had no trouble setting the pace as they paddled in the direction of the smaller island. "I take it you've been in a canoe before. You're pretty handy with an oar."

"Girl Scouts. It was the only extra curricular activity I was allowed to do growing up besides sports. My father wanted me to learn to be useful in the woods and my mother insisted I do it while being with other girls."

"Only child?" he asked.

"Only girl."

He nodded his head. "Makes sense. Fathers can be overprotective and overbearing."

"Is that knowledge from experience?"

Diego thought about her question while watching the smooth strokes she made in the water. Strong, beautiful and feisty. The list of things he liked about her was getting longer and longer.

"I see it in the pack all the time. Girl pups are pretty rare, so when they do come along they are coddled and protected beyond necessity."

"No children yourself?" she whispered the question, full knowing he would still hear it.

"No." His answer was both gruff and abrupt. Hopefully she got the message he didn't want to talk about it.

They continued the rest of the way in silence, each scanning the island as they got close and not seeing anything out of the ordinary.

The light he'd seen from the point had disappeared. Maybe it had been a trick of the moon shining on something colorful.

When they hit land she scrambled out of the canoe and he followed suit before lifting the canoe and stowing it inside the tree line so it wouldn't be spotted.

"It's really quiet here. It seems deserted," she whispered.

"Too much so. The forest is rarely a silent place. It could be quiet because I'm here now or it might be something else."

"Because you're a wolf."

It wasn't a question but the tone of her statement made him uneasy. The word wolf didn't come easy.

"You really hate us, don't you?"

Her head whipped around and her widened eyes fixed on his. "I don't even know what I'm supposed to say to that."

"The truth," he suggested.

"Well, the truth is I don't know what to think anymore. You're the first shifter I've ever encountered who wasn't trying to kill me. Although I fully expected it when I was first tackled on the beach. You and your brothers were so angry."

"Rightfully so. You shot Dante. It's kind of hard to keep a level head when your brother narrowly escapes death."

She rolled her eyes. "I don't know how many times I have to tell you that if I wanted him dead he would be. I could have made that shot with my eyes closed and one arm tied behind my back."

"So you keep saying."

She threw her arms up in frustration and blew out a hard breath before she turned away and started up the beach. "Let's just get this over with. The sooner we find no one out here the sooner we can leave."

A loud snap sounded from in front of them.

"I don't think we're alone..."

Allison fought the nerves taking flight in her stomach. If he was out there they should both be worried. She wasn't sure what to expect but she had a hunch it wasn't good. Which is why she'd come prepared.

The sounds ahead of them disappeared and she took off to follow them.

"Hey," Diego called behind her.

She didn't have time to stop and chat with him anymore. She had to find her brother. He was in danger from their family *and* these werewolves and she wasn't about to let either faction kill him.

There had to be a way to save him.

She ran harder, ignoring the branches scraping at her arms and face as she single-mindedly followed the subtle signs of a trail left behind by someone moving fast. Freshly broken branches, depressed leaves, and compacted soil all made it obvious someone had been here watching her and Diego come on the island.

Not that Diego was far behind her. She didn't have a hope in hell of outrunning him, but if he followed from the rear then there was a chance she could get between her brother Brody and the wolf Diego before they attacked each other.

A snarl not far in front of her brought her to a screeching halt. There was a very large tan wolf now standing in her path and his eyes glowed yellow while he continued to growl at her.

At her back, another growl snarled was her only warning before the sound of bones popping and breaking filled her ears.

Afraid to take her eyes from the animal in front of her, she didn't move.

"Brody?"

The animal took a step forward and she got a closer-than-she-ever-wanted-to look at sharp teeth barely contained under the wolf's lips.

She held out her hands. "I'm not here to hurt you. But we need to—"

Before she finished her sentence the man/wolf behind her sailed over her head and landed gracefully on the forest floor in front of her.

"No!" she screamed

She'd officially lost the only advantage she had, and if Diego hurt him or vice versa...

Teeth bared, the two animals circled each other. They were going to attack any second and probably kill each other before she could stop them. She had to do something.

Allison bent over and lifted her pant leg and grabbed the tiny gun from the holster still strapped to her calf. How it had been missed when she was tackled on the beach was nothing short of a miracle.

She aimed it toward the two wolves and stared down the sights. Now she only had to decide which one to shoot.

Before she could pick, they took the decision away from her when Diego attacked Brody in a blur of movement and vicious growls that scraped along her spine far worse than any nails on a chalkboard.

Fur flew as they wrestled each other to the ground and took turns biting at each other. Diego's nearly all black fur stood out in contrast to the much lighter coat of Brody's. If they weren't actually trying to kill each other, she might stand back and admire the beauty of the creatures in front of her.

She filed that strange thought away for further examination when there wasn't a fight to the death going on in front of her. Werewolves were supposed to be her enemies, not subjects of her admiration. This island was getting to her and she didn't like it.

Diego twisted in Brody's grasp and came up under her brother's throat. With sudden clarity she could see the vulnerable spot that Diego was after. She moved the gun to the left and sighted in on both of them. But the way they fought and moved it was really difficult to zone in on either of them. They were both lightning fast.

Brody slashed outward, snagging his claws into the other wolf's side. Diego scrambled backward, twisting his body to pry the razor sharp claws loose. But Brody knew how to fight as dirty as they came and he managed to keep hold of Diego by sinking his teeth into the wolf's shoulder.

The snarling howls of both animals filled Allison's mind with pain. They were both moving so fast it was hard to tell who was doing what to whom. The fight became a blur of snarls and growls that filled the air.

Then Diego grabbed her brother and jerked him away from his shoulder. That was when she saw the bright red sheen of blood coating one side of Brody.

With the horror of the situation staring her straight in the face she tightened her stance and aimed the gun. One way or another she had to stop this. She only hoped she hit the right one.

Her brother recovered and renewed his attack, knocking Diego across the small clearing and into the tree. With a ferocious growl he followed that up by launching himself on top of Diego's wolf.

For Allison, instinct kicked in. She whipped her gun around, took a shallow breath and squeezed the trigger while looking straight down the sight. The gun went off and her arms jerked from the recoil.

Startled, both wolves turned her way. They scrambled apart and for a moment she thought she'd missed as they turned back to each other, both ready to finish the fight.

Then Brody stumbled. He turned and looked at her, howling in her direction. Diego followed suit.

The pain of that look stabbed her squarely in the chest.

Her brother sat down on his haunches, his howls growing weaker until they sounded more like human whimpers. Bones popped and muscles stretched. One minute he was the wolf and the next he was her beloved brother falling over on his side.

She rushed forward, dropping the gun. "Brody. Oh my God. It is you."

"You shot me."

"I had to do something. You were going to kill him."

"So? That's no reason to shoooot meeee." The tranquilizer she'd shot him with was beginning to take hold.

"Don't be such a baby about it. I think we have bigger issues than a pinch and some drug aftereffects."

"Yeah, like who he is and how you know him," a familiar voice growled behind her.

"Back off, mother fucker. I may look down for the count, but you haven't seen anything yet." The drugs hadn't done much to take the edge from his attitude.

"Shut up, Brody." And of course he didn't listen, because he never did.

"You touch one hair on my sister's head and I'll kill you twice just for the fun of it." Her brother's threat seemed menacing until he gave her one last look and promptly passed out.

"So... Aren't we the little secret keeper?" Diego appeared in her peripheral vision as naked as her brother. She kept her eyes forward doing her damndest not to take a peek. This was not the time or the place to deal with how his state of undress might affect her.

"Knew it was something." He bent down and picked up the gun, nudging Brody with his foot. "Clever girl keeping this hidden."

"Leave him alone. You've done enough, don't you think?" Guilt washed over her at her brother's predicament. He'd gone well past simply bitten.

"Me?" he asked. "I was fighting to save you."

Allison guffawed. "I don't need your saving. I just needed to find my brother and keep him alive until I figure out how to help him."

"Alive for what? What are you planning to do with him now that you have him? It's time for some answers, Allison."

Maybe it was, but she still wasn't sure whether she could trust him or not. Her gut said yes, while her head played devil's advocate. He was one of *them*. And a lifetime of training couldn't be wiped away in a single night. But neither could this sense of something being very wrong about all of this. He was trying to shake up her entire belief system. Either way it was driving her crazy.

"I barely know you, so how can I trust you with anything, let alone this?" She waved her hand over her brother. "I've spent my entire life believing one thing." She looked up at him. "One thing. Don't you get that? I have to either do what I'm told and kill you both or..."

"Or what?" he asked, crouching down next to her.

Tears she would never shed pooled in her eyes as the pain of truth lashed against her fragile heart. "Become the hunted," she whispered.

Diego tried to digest her words as he picked up her brother and trudged him back to where Brody had set up camp. It actually wasn't much more than a lean to shelter and a campfire. Not that a wolf technically needed much more, and as a newly turned wolf he likely spent more time on all fours than he did in his current human form.

Grabbing an extra pair of pants from a nearby backpack Diego found as part of Brody's camp, he slid them over his legs and fastened them at his hips. They were a little big, making the fabric ride low. Not that he cared. He had little issue with his naked form, and only covered himself for her sake.

His body vibrated with fury over the situation between Allison and her brother. It pissed him off more than the fact the hunters and their distorted ways had managed to infect his island. Two of them on Devils Point felt like overkill. Even if one of them was now a wolf.

They were in a Catch 22 situation here and they all knew it. If she was allowed to leave, she'd come back eventually with more of her kind. The carnage that would follow would get ugly, but more importantly their secret would be out and they'd have to relocate.

He also had the situation with the brother. He looked and acted like a newly turned wolf on the verge of losing his mind. If he was feral, there was a high probability the pack would have to put him down for the safety of himself and others.

This was the danger of turning humans. It didn't always take. Especially without a mate bond.

And then there was his third problem. Allison was his fated mate. As it turned out, the hokey bullshit that he'd "just know" had turned out true and that annoyed him to no end. That meant the wolf inside him would literally do anything to keep her close.

Anything. Including defend her life to the death.

The man on the other hand... Diego held his head in his hands and took a long, slow breath. Years ago he'd tried to bond with a shifter female. It didn't take. She'd turned her back on him and left town leaving him with nothing but a Dear John letter and a messed up head to show for his time.

His jaw hardened. That betrayal to him and the pack still burned deep. And it served a purpose. Reminding him that some bonds made him weak. Something he refused to be again.

Diego back tracked to the mouth of the clearing and searched through the brush until he found remnants of his pants. He dug into the pocket and pulled out his still intact cell phone. He turned it on and checked for signal. Weak. But maybe just enough to get a text message through.

He began tapping out a message to Creed.

"What are you doing?" Allison asked.

"Calling for a pick up."

"Why? You and I can handle this. I don't think it's a good idea for others to know what's happening."

He frowned at her. "That's where you're wrong. Your brother is a lot more dangerous than you know."

"What part of I need to keep him alive did you not get? I don't want anyone else touching him."

This time her feist did not humor him. "I got the message just fine. I'm not suggesting we kill him--yet. Now you need to let me do what I do best. You don't know shifters as well as you think you do, remember? Besides, my first idea is to *not* kill him, but to try and save him. He was bitten and the least we can do is try to get him through the transition."

She sat stunned, not responding.

"In order to do that I've got to get him somewhere safe where he can't hurt you, me or anyone else. Got it?"

The resignation that crossed her face tore at his defenses. He didn't want to make his mate unhappy. Only do what was best for her without compromising their safety. His concern for her brother was and always would be, secondary.

He cupped her cheek, savoring the soft skin he wanted to explore. "I give you my word, nothing will happen to him you don't know about. Creed and Sawyer will keep us apprised of his progress. If a decision has to be made about his welfare, then I will inform you."

For a moment she turned her face into his hand and pressed her nose to his calloused skin. "What about me? What am I supposed to do during all this? I can't go home and just leave my brother's life in your hands."

"You'll stay with me."

She pulled back. "Uhm...Excuse me? Why on earth would I do that?"

"I can't just let you go. There are complications. Until we figure all of this out, you can stay at my place as my guest."

"I don't know about that. I shot your brother, remember? Your pack is not going to want to see me, let alone embrace me."

He tucked a strand of blonde hair behind her ear. "Whatever agreement you and I come to, the pack will go along with. You can't worry about them right now. We will likely need your help with your brother and his humanity."

She frowned. "What's the catch? From my experience if it seems too good to be true then it is."

He sighed, blowing out a hard breath. "You're too young to be this jaded."

"Well, you already told me you wanted to have sex with me. Is that what this is about? And I'm not that young."

"You worried?" he asked, some of his frustration giving way to the need to make her happy. "I am irresistible after all."

That got a smile from her and it went straight to his cock. Wanting to get inside her was no joke. But he wasn't going to coerce her. Although some gentle nudges or using all of the seduction tools in his arsenal wasn't out of the question. "Relax, Allison. Whatever happens or doesn't happen is up to you. I'm not going to force you into anything."

"What if I want to leave?"

"You don't."

"But what if I did? What then?"

Diego gripped her shoulders and hauled her to her feet. "Stop grilling me on things with no relevance to this situation. You want to be close to your brother and I want you close to me. There's nothing else to discuss."

"You're very bossy. Do you have a thing for being in charge that I need to know about?" The words were serious but her eyes were full of mischief when she said them. It made him groan.

"I'm a shifter. So staying in my home is not going to be like hanging out with some human. I won't be coy or play games, I'll tell you what I expect and want. Then you can decide if you want it too. Of course, you *can* disagree with me, but expect to be worn down until you get my point."

She rolled her eyes. "Are you trying to convince me to stay or go? It's a little hard to tell with the picture you paint."

He pulled her close and tipped her head back with his finger at her chin. "Oh you'll stay. Of that I have no doubt. But more importantly, and this isn't going to change no matter what happens, I do still plan to fuck you."

Her reaction to his intentions made her mouth drop open again and he took advantage of the opportunity. He leaned forward and captured her mouth with his, his hands moving to cradle the sides of her face.

The initial touch was light, but after a stunned moment Diego deepened the kiss, turning it desperate for them both.

SEVEN

Too shocked to think it through, Allison allowed him to take control by opening to him. Diego's mouth was hot, making her fall all the easier. She welcomed the firm strokes of his tongue as he tasted her and she tasted him back.

When the world began to spin, she grabbed his shoulders and held on. She knew he was spectacular to look at but she hadn't counted on the sensation of her hands on hard muscles stretched beneath silky skin.

Heat rushed through her before she could stop it, where it quickly thawed her resistance to a man supposedly forbidden to her. He didn't taste forbidden. He tasted decadent. Exotic. And better than chocolate.

Even better was the way Diego held her. His grip was tight, harder than necessary and should have had every alarm bell in her head going off. Yet, the possessive nature in which he claimed that kiss made her flower against him. The heady sensations went straight to her head, making his demanding touch far better than any before him.

The wild kiss continued as he pulled her tight, ensuring they were plastered together from shoulder to hip. At that point her brain shut down as need and desire caught fire and began to consume her.

Every inch of her body heated to the point of no return. She simply craved more. That's all she could think of. More of this kiss. More of him. Whatever it took. It could NOT stop.

Need so fierce she couldn't breathe slammed into her. Her hands wound their way up to his shoulders and neck and into the silky strands of his dark hair, where she grabbed at them desperately and drew him closer in every way.

He groaned into her mouth, turning the kiss between them downright savage. Tongue, teeth--they all collided as the unleashed need coiled tight in her belly and threatened to burst free with almost no other stimulation.

But it wasn't just desire he drew from her. Something sparked in her chest and the well of emotion she kept locked up tight began to crack. It was as if he was drawing the emotions out of her, and she was helpless to make it stop.

The first of many of her worries floated to the top. The pain of being captured by a madman was never far from the surface and it was easy to see why.

Diego growled, sliding his hands down to her buttocks and squeezing at the same time pulling her closer. Taking that memory from her and locking it away.

The worry for her brother came next as did the fear of what their family might do to them if she didn't bring him home—dead or alive. She jerked in his arms unable to understand how or why this was happening. Or how to make it stop.

If she wanted him too...

He ignored her reaction and held her tight, giving her some much needed comfort in the safe harbor of his arms. For a moment she believed that maybe, just maybe, everything could actually work out. Her life until now had been nothing but chaos and fate hadn't been kind in the past. Did that maybe mean it was finally time for something good to happen?

Keep me safe.

The words floated through her mind before she could stop them. Diego broke the kiss and stared down at her, his breaths harsh and uneasy between them.

"Always," he said.

She was panting as well, making it difficult to understand what he said. But there was something inexplainable about him that made her accept him and his offer for the simplicity of what it meant.

When he pressed his forehead to hers, she melted against him. A sense of calm washed over her. While it didn't erase the unease that still plagued her, it did give her a sense that this man needed her as much as she needed him. Her instincts practically screamed this at her. How was she supposed to fight a mysterious sensation and why would she want to?

The more she tried to puzzle it out, the harder it was to see anything that made sense. Instincts were one thing, but this seemed like a whole different level of things. It was almost as if she could feel him actually under her skin, working his way towards her heart. But that was impossible. They barely knew each other. By now her body was shaking and he cupped the back of her head and leaned her into his shoulder.

"It's okay, beautiful. You can't fight it. It's nature. It wants what it wants. Come home with me. Let me keep you safe while we wait to see if Creed and Sawyer can help your brother. We'll figure out our next move together as it's meant to be."

Part of her still worried about Brody's safety, but something deeper urged her to go with this man. That it was the right decision. That she AND her brother would be safe this way...

"Okay," she finally whispered. "I'll go with you. But only because Brody will need me nearby so he doesn't have to worry." That was a lie and they both knew it. Him because he seemed to understand what was happening, and her because Brody was not the only reason she wanted to go.

Diego kissed her again, his tongue breaching her mouth once more.

She sighed, sinking into him. This would be okay. It was only for a little while. There would be plenty of time to figure this out later.

EIGHT

Shortly after Creed and Sawyer arrived to scoop up her brother, Diego took Allison back to his house. While everything was fairly quiet he scented the beginnings of breakfast.

"Smells like someone is cooking. You hungry?"

She nodded.

"Good. Let me get you settled and then I'll see about getting you fed. He led her down to the finished basement and opened the guest room door. Although calling this the guest room was quite a stretch. Inside there was a small bed made from steel with a thin mattress, an even tinier bathroom in the corner that could be closed off but not locked, and a television built into the wall behind Plexiglas to keep it safe from any angry shifters they needed to house.

"Why does this look like a prison cell?" she asked.

"It's a multipurpose room. Whatever the occasion, it works."

"And does this occasion include locking me in here?"

"I wouldn't say lock you in per se. It's just that the door automatically locks when you close it. But no worries, I'm going straight up stairs to get your food and right back down here again. I'm not leaving you."

She looked skeptical, her raised eyebrows saying it all.

He backed away quickly before she had time to get defensive and start a debate. "Promise, I'll be right back." He slipped out the door and closed it firmly behind him. A little to keep her in and a lot to keep others out. Until he had time to explain the situation to his pack, it wouldn't do anyone good to find her down here.

He took the stairs three steps at a time until he entered the main dining/kitchen/living room space. There he found Faith, Damien, Rebel and Dante all gathered around the table in his dining room.

The table was covered with every kind of breakfast food known to man and his stomach growled. He eyed the piles of meat and contemplated where he would start. Ultimately, he decided a lot of everything. Whatever Allison didn't eat, he'd finish for her.

"I hope you plan to save some for me," he said. He hopped into one of the empty chairs and grabbed a plate. After picking out about ten slices of bacon, he dug into the pile of eggs and glanced up to find them all staring at him.

"What?" he asked.

"Oh, I don't know," Damien started. "Last time we saw you, you were walking away with our captured hunter and no one has seen you since. Where is she?"

"In the basement. I've been interrogating her." He stuffed two pieces of sausage in his mouth and reached for the pancakes.

He glanced over at Rebel and Dante to find them staring at him while continuing to touch each other. "So you two finally did it, huh?" Not that it wasn't obvious. The bonding pheromones cloaking them were still fresh and fucking with his brain.

He took a deep breath and focused on the food in front of him. He'd been too busy to eat and he had some catching up to do.

"That's it? You're not going to tell us what happened with her?" Rebel asked.

He shrugged. "Sure. Her name is Allison Fox and she's from Seattle. Her brother Brody was supposedly attacked and bitten by a wolf either here on the island or nearby. Now he's missing and she is hunting him and prepared to take out any shifter who gets in her way. So... Needless to say, I've got her locked up until we can do something about her brother who is our rogue wolf."

Dante's disbelieving eyebrow popped up. "It took you that long to get that little?"

"More or less." What was he supposed to say? He wasn't about to tell them the truth. At least, not all of it. They only had a few hours of mating season to go and then he could wipe this mess clean.

No one needed to know he was addicted to a woman trying to find a way to kill him.

"Did you forget something?"

Everyone at the table jumped up at the voice behind them, plates and food clattering to the floor. Dante and Damien started growling, shoving their women behind them.

Fear jumped into Allison's eyes as she realized she'd walked into a sticky situation. She held up her hands in surrender. "I'm sorry, I didn't mean to startle you. I thought Diego would have told you I was here by now."

She glared at him like venom darts were going to shoot his way any second.

"Diego, what the hell is going on?" Dante hissed.

"Yes, brother. Tell us what is happening—" Damien's head shot up. "And why the hell does she smell like—"

"Whoa, there's no need to get your hackles in a twist. Any of you," Diego shouted. "Allison and I have come to an agreement. So chill."

"But she's a hunter," Rebel said.

"She was. Or is. But more importantly, her brother is one of us. Although he's on the edge of feral."

"Then we need to get out there and find him before he hurts someone."

"Already done. Got him pinned down last night out on Deadman's Island where he was hiding and turned him over to Creed. He should be safely locked up by now."

"What?" they all yelled, except for Allison. This situation was about to blow.

"You mind if I grab breakfast while you all work this out?" Allison took a tentative step toward the table.

"Of course." Faith jumped into motion and Damien had to practically pin her to the wall to stop her.

"You can't be around her right now?"

"Why not?" she asked.

"Because she's a damned hunter and if she comes at you, you're going to kill her. That's why." Damien's anger came spewing out. "I'm not putting that on you. If she needs to be killed it's going to be by me."

Faith must have sensed Damien's desperation when it came to her safety as she quickly moved away and safely behind his brothers.

"I'm not going to do anything, I swear. I just want food. I'm starving."

"Help yourself," said Faith, without coming out from behind her mate.

"I want answers." Dante said, looking like he was about to blow.

"Allison, I thought you were staying downstairs." Diego interrupted.

"Locked up down there you mean?" She shrugged. "Got a phobia about being locked up. Which means there isn't a door made I can't find my way around."

"Girls got skills," Rebel said.

"I'd say." Damien said, still not sounding thrilled about the turn of events. "Might as well let her eat."

"Thank you," Allison said. She grabbed one of the empty plates still sitting on the table and picked some bacon from one of the intact platters.

Diego watched her closely. She seemed normal to the naked eye, but something seemed off. Her foot tapped against the chair leg and he detected a slight tremble in her arms as she ate.

"What's wrong with her?" Faith whispered. Too low for Allison to hear but well within hearing of the rest of them.

Diego didn't answer. His mate was in some sort of distress and the wolf inside was beginning to complain about it. Fur sprouted along his arms and his hearing and eyesight sharpened. He imagined his eyes changed color as well.

"Diego, what did you do?" Damien asked. "Her scent has changed." He sniffed the air. "You didn't bite her, but something happened."

"All I did was kiss her. She was fine when I left her downstairs." His words came out rough from the partial change.

"You're playing with fire, brother."

Diego looked at Dante. "Tell me something I don't already know."

"If I didn't know better I would think your human was in the throes of mating frenzy. She smells ripe."

Shit.

Damien shook his head. "We're out of here. I've got to get Faith home before this mess triggers her wolf. We don't need her tearing through the place trying to figure out why she's out of control."

Dante shook his head. "We're out too. I'll head over to check on the rogue. Find out what his status is. Call us when you get this situation under control. You know what you have to do."

Diego nodded at his brothers as they filed out of the house. He couldn't focus on anything but Allison and the source of her distress.

When she looked up at him he saw the pain in her eyes she could no longer hide.

"Do you have any aspirin," she asked, looking around. "Where did everyone go?"

"They left, beautiful. You were scaring them."

"I told you they weren't going to be okay with me. No pack wants a hunter in their midst."

"That's true. But you're much more than a hunter now."

She looked up, the question already in her eyes. "What are you talking about?"

He sighed. There was no getting around telling her now. Her pain was killing him.

"Tell me how you're feeling?" he asked.

"I'm fine. Just a headache."

"You're shaky. I can see it."

"Low blood sugar. I needed food."

He frowned knowing it was far more than that. "I don't doubt you were hungry, but eating isn't working is it?"

Her fork froze mid air. "I don't know what you mean."

He listened to her heart rate increase. "I'm not sure how it happened, but I think we've triggered a mating frenzy." His body was certainly feeling it. He was painfully hard and fighting it continued to make it worse.

"What the hell are you talking about? My being here is doing something to your mating thingy?"

Diego laughed low and slow. "You're so damned cute it hurts." He took the fork out of her hand and pulled her out of her seat. "Come on. I'll get you some aspirin, but I don't think it's going to help."

"Why not? Are you a doctor too?"

"Hardly. But I can recognize the symptoms of mating season. I've been through it enough to know. Fortunately, in your case it won't last long. The moon will begin to wane soon."

She stopped and pulled free from his hold. "What on earth are you talking about? Are you suggesting I'm in some sort of mating thing? What kind of nonsense is that? I'm not like you, or have you forgotten that I'm one hundred percent human?"

He shook his head. "Nope. That is something I could never forget. You don't smell anything like a wolf."

She scrunched up her face. "Do I want to know what I smell like?" She held up her hand. "No, don't tell me. I want to hear more about this mating nonsense you've got in your head."

For a moment his brain was stuck on the fact she smelled like roses on a warm summer night mixed with the fresh salty air of the ocean. But he'd save that information for another day.

"It's simple really," he said. "You're my fated mate and as such and due to proximity it's triggered a frenzy for not just me but you too."

Allison stared at him like he'd grown a second head. What he was saying made no sense. She remembered what little he'd mentioned about the mating bond, but she couldn't believe he'd take it so far as to include her. That was outrageous.

"I get that you want to have sex with me," she said. "But you don't have to take it that far to get it. I was already halfway there."

He reached up and brushed his thumbs across her temples. "And you have no idea how much I like that. Keeping it simple would have been preferred. Unfortunately, it doesn't change the truth. Most of what you're feeling is because mother nature dictates it."

"I don't believe that." She swayed into his hands, now massaging her head, which felt really really good. "I don't mean to discount your culture in any way, but I don't believe it applies to me. If my body and heart craves yours it goes far beyond some easy magical connection. Maybe it's lust and maybe it's more. But I'm not going to discount it down to nothing."

Diego leaned forward and pressed his lips to hers in a soft and touching kiss. The feather light touch made her stomach somersault.

More. The call in her head was more urgent than before.

"You're too sweet for a man like me. Hell, you're too sweet for the life you lead. Judging others based solely on their species doesn't suit you. You're better than that."

She leaned forward and pressed her forehead to his. "I know. But it's all I've ever known. At this point it feels hardwired and I don't know if I can learn to be anything else."

"You can," he insisted. "I'm certain."

She closed her eyes and drew in a deep breath. If she didn't already want to sleep with him, his tenderness now sealed the deal for her.

"C'mon," he said. "You need sleep. If we can get you through this, then by tonight things should be a lot less painful."

"Because the mating thing will be over?" Not that she was starting to believe, she just liked hearing him talk to her.

He nodded, grabbing her hand and pulling her toward a bedroom instead of the basement. They walked into a large room with blinds drawn making the room cool and semi dark.

In the center of the room sat a large king sized bed loaded down with big pillows and a comforter still twisted from the last time he used it. And his scent was everywhere. Cedar and smoke and earth...

The bed looked so good she wanted to fall down face first and pass out. Except she really needed a shower so she could wash some of the stink off of her. He'd said something about how she smelled and she shuddered to think how bad it might be. Her single-minded focus on finding her brother hadn't left a lot of time for personal grooming.

"Shower?" she asked.

"Sure. Bathroom's through there. Towels are under the sink. I'll get a t-shirt you can put on after."

Allison followed his instructions and slipped through the bathroom door. To her surprise she discovered an amazing space worthy of any spa she might imagine. It consisted of a soaker tub in the corner, a double vanity near the door and a spacious custom tiled shower that looked like it could accommodate a lot more than two people. And there were multiple shower heads from above and the walls.

She wasted no time in getting her clothes off and jumping into the multi head spray of the shower. The hot water sluicing over her skin felt so damn good she almost cried. There was a good chance she was never getting out. Or leaving...

She shook that insane thought free. As soon as she got things settled with Brody, she would have to return home. Her family would be waiting for answers.

She lathered a fresh washcloth with Diego's spicy soap and breathed deep. It reminded her so much of the man who claimed she was his mate she nearly dropped to her knees. She'd always known scent as a powerful tool, but this wasn't like that. It was more akin to taking a bottle of kerosene and pouring it over her body just before lighting it on fire.

She swayed forward, keening as she moved. How could this be happening to her? Her skin tightened, her breasts ached and the moisture between her legs had nothing to do with shower.

The door slammed open. "What's wrong?"

She screamed, clutching the tiny washcloth to her chest and shoving her hand between her legs to cover more.

The door swung open and Diego stepped in fully clothed. "It's worse?" he asked.

She nodded, unable to speak. It definitely didn't make sense.

He pulled her into his arms and cradled her head to his chest. "Take a deep breath and tell me what happened." His free hand went to her back and stroked up and down.

"I—I don't know. I was just trying to wash. But the soap. It smells so much like you. I don't know, it got to me."

"I'm so sorry, beautiful. I wish I could make this go away."

She lifted her head and met his gaze. "But you can, can't you? If this is some sort of mating thing, isn't that the point?"

He nodded. "Yes, it is. But I'm not letting it go down like this. Rational decisions are not made in the heat of the moment."

She placed her head back on his hard chest, forehead down. "I think rational is overrated."

He chuckled, soothing his hands down her back. "That's the heat talking."

"What if it's not? What if this is really what I want?" Maybe it was lust and maybe it wasn't, but for the first time in her life she felt comfortable in her own skin.

"I really hope it is. But I think we should wait."

The hesitation in his voice chipped another piece of armor from around her heart. If he felt half of what she did then the kind of restraint he had to employ was impressive.

But it didn't have to be like that. What was the point of either of us suffering?

"Diego, we're not kids. We can handle this. I can handle this." She freed her hands from between them and cupped his face, studying the angular bone structure of his face that made him one of the most handsome men she'd ever met. "You probably should remove these wet clothes though."

Not waiting for a response, in case he planned to reject her, she lifted onto her tippy toes and kissed him. Not just any kiss, mind you, she poured everything she had into that slow kiss making sure he got the full extent of what she meant.

If her bare breasts rubbed against his hard chest in the process, well, that simply couldn't be helped.

When he slid his hands down to her buttocks and lifted, she smiled into his mouth. It didn't make a lot of sense that she would fall for him so hard and so fast, but it was there whether he wanted to admit it or not.

Maybe there was some mystical force at work, and maybe there wasn't. I wasn't sure that was possible, but even if it was I still believed it was mostly because of him. He was fair and charming, protective and sexy, and he thought she was beautiful.

She pulled free from the kiss and whispered, "I'm hungry."

TEN

Diego groaned. The wet bundle of heat currently wrapped around him was too much for him to resist. It hurt him to know that she needed something he could easily give.

He lifted her and turned, pressing her backside into the shower wall. With the jets coming from multiple directions, water poured over them. He leaned in and licked some of the moisture from her neck before nipping the tender skin lightly with his teeth.

No breaking the skin, but he'd leave a mark nonetheless.

He'd barely had time to register her nudity when he first entered the shower, but now every glorious inch was plastered to his front and he wanted to explore.

Diego nuzzled between her breasts, admiring their perfect size. He drew back until her nipples appeared, puckered and ready for his mouth. Too tempting not to taste, he swiped his tongue across one peak before drawing the next in his mouth.

Holy shit she tasted good.

Allison gasped, her hands tightening on his shoulders. He moaned, taking more plump breast in his mouth. As he moved back and forth, giving equal attention, he realized part of him wanted to do this all day. Except there was a hell of a lot more he wanted to get his hands and mouth on.

While his body heated the more he explored, he noticed that some of the pain from unmet desire had begun to recede. He had his beautiful mate right where he needed her.

He didn't fully understand how she got so affected without a bite, but at the moment he not only didn't care, he was grateful. To miss out on this would be Mother Nature's cruelest trick to date.

Using his tongue, Diego made a trail that started between her breasts and moved down to her navel. He teased the indentation and smiled when her stomach muscles clenched. Now squatting, he grabbed her thighs and nudged them apart, revealing the sweet scent of her arousal that already intoxicated him.

He leaned forward and placed a chaste kiss on the neatly trimmed spot between her legs a moment before he slid his tongue over her clit.

Allison moaned, tilting her hips so he had a better angle, giving him an unspoken invitation to continue. He chuckled, the sound drowned out by the jets of water still pelting her skin. Diego grabbed her hips to steady her and moved in to get his fill of the perfection that was his mate.

When her body sagged, he applied more pressure to keep her upright as he slid his mouth over her opening and teased the succulent flesh waiting for him.

Her hands went into his hair, fingers tightening on the strands. She tried to guide him where she wanted more, but he was way ahead of her. He pressed his tongue inside her in leisure thrusts designed to drive her to the brink.

It would never be enough for either of them until he filled her with his cock. For now though, this would do.

"Diego," she whined. "Please."

Despite her pleas, he didn't sway from his plan. Instead he savored her, enjoying this first moment with his mate and her heat. She tasted so—hell he had no words for how wonderful it was. But he was getting drunk on her with every passing second.

The sting of her hands pulling tighter on his hair only suffused him with satisfaction as he looked up to find her rolling her head back and forth on the shower tiles.

Impressed with her response, he moved his tongue faster and faster across her slick skin. She cried out as her body began to convulse with pleasure and he drank in every moment.

Watching her come was a sight to behold and one he'd never forget no matter what tomorrow brought them.

When he was satisfied that his mate was sated, he rose and stared down at her. Her eyes fluttered between open and closed and her gorgeous mouth looked ripe as hell.

So he kissed her.

When she responded by opening for him and grabbing his shoulders, he took them both deeper, looking for that hunger that still nagged at them both.

Her hands went crazy, roaming over his still clothed body and he cursed the fact he didn't bother to remove them earlier. Not that something like wet jeans deterred her. Her hands were at the fastenings working them roughly until she got them open.

He started to protest and she ignored him, her hand diving inside and encircling his erection.

Holy fuck. He couldn't breath.

She stumbled for a moment more and then he was free. Long, hard and standing out straight to her belly. Apparently determined to see this through, she again gave him no chance to stop her before her hand was stroking up and down his length.

He wrenched free from her mouth and gulped for air. She was squeezing and pulling in perfect tandem and his mind threatened to explode from the ecstasy of each tug.

Diego grabbed his pants and yanked them out of the way so she could get a better grip and began thrusting his hips to get more.

"Holy hell, Allison. You are a beautiful genius. So damned beautiful."

She smiled at him and quickened her strokes before leaning in to attack his chest and neck with her teeth. Each little nip ignited a jolt of pleasure that went straight to his cock, the intensity almost too much to bear. His need for her went so deep inside him he knew he would never get it out. This woman would be his until the end of his days.

He grabbed the wall and braced for the oncoming explosion as he thrust into her fist as hard as he could. She was so warm, and smelled so good. Not to mention he still had the sweet taste of her lingering on his tongue...

"Allison!"

He grabbed her by the shoulders and pulled her tight against him. He thrusted and came as if he was inside her, making her see what it would be like when he finally fucked her.

Allison smiled, her eyes flashing hot and then she bit him a lot harder than before.

Diego lifted his head and released the wolf, who howled so loud it probably shook the windows. Everything about this moment was more beautiful and sensual than he ever dreamed it could be. There was no pain. Only joy that he had found her. It now seemed painfully obvious that he could never let her go. The way she made him feel whole was unlike anything he'd experienced before. In that moment, with the water still raining down on them and his dick in her hand, he felt more at peace than he remembered.

Except he did have to let her go for now. She still had a decision to come to when she was not so hungry. Diego kissed her and held her tight for a few minutes more. He really didn't want this moment to end.

"Diego, I want more," she whispered against his skin.

"I know, beautiful. I do too. But we have to wait. To get inside you now, I don't think I could stop myself from biting you and making our connection permanent."

"I think I'm okay with that."

The wolf growled in his head, warning him not to disappoint the mate. But the human in him wouldn't allow her to make that decision while need still clawed at her gut.

Not that he wasn't as greedy as the wolf. He had to use an exorbitant amount of restraint to let her go and step out of the shower.

"Tell me how you feel after a good night's sleep. If you still feel the same way tomorrow, no one will be able to stop me," he said.

"I really don't think a few hours are going to make any difference, but I find it extremely gallant of you to make us wait."

Diego chuckled and reached for a towel. "Remember that thought. You'll soon learn that gallant is hardly in my vocabulary."

He began drying her off, enjoying this moment almost as much as his orgasm. Caring for her, admiring her luscious body... Damn she was one fine woman.

Once she was taken care of and she began dressing in his t-shirt, he quickly ripped the rest of his soaking wet clothes off and quickly dried. Only when he heard a soft gasp did he look up to discover her watching him.

"What?" he asked.

"You're still hard."

He smiled, enjoying the hell out of her shocked look. "It happens. During mating season especially it's not uncommon to come several times a day."

Her face flushed bright red. "Seriously?"

He nodded and tossed his towel into the laundry hamper. "Now off to bed you, or I might not be able to resist showing you."

She smiled and looked at him with hunger, but fortunately followed his command and headed back into the bedroom, wiggling her lush ass the whole way.

"If I'm sleeping in here, where will you sleep? I don't want to take your bed."

He smiled at her as she climbed under the covers.

"I think this bed is more than big enough for the two of us wouldn't you agree?"

She nodded, already looking a little sleepy as she snuggled into the pillows. "I really like your house you know."

"Thank you. I'm pretty fond of it too. Took a long time to get it right." He climbed in the opposite side and rolled toward her. He didn't think he'd sleep a wink if he tried to hold her, but nothing could stop him from resting his hand on her hip.

Eventually, the air around them settled and both their heart rates slowed. It had been a long day and night and he was beginning to feel the fatigue take over.

"Allison?"

"Mmmhmm?"

"Why did you shoot my brother?" It was the one question still nagging at him. If she had no intention of killing him, then why?

She rolled over and looked up at him. "I was feeling desperate. After weeks of trying to hunt my brother, I was no closer to finding him. I feared I was running out of time. So I took a risk and shot at your pack, hoping that when you captured me, I'd find out something—anything that would help me find Brody."

"That was quite a risk."

She shrugged. "He's my brother. I'd do anything to save him."

Diego thought about this. Her plan had been insane at best. But it had worked. It seemed his mate was going to keep him on his toes.

"Diego?"

"Yes, beautiful?"

"Tell me about her."

"Who?"

She touched his cheek and he turned and kissed her hand. "The first woman you tried to take as a mate. What happened?"

He closed his eyes. This was not the conversation he ever wanted to have with her. But she answered his question so he owed her the same. "She left me not too long after we agreed to bond. When I went after her to bring her home she shot me."

Allison gasped. "Why in the world?"

"That is the million dollar question I guess. And one I never got the answer to. I died the night she shot me."

"I'm so sorry," she said.

"No, I mean that literally. She nicked my heart and it quit beating. If not for my brother and his EMT skills, I wouldn't be here today."

"What a bitch. Where is she now?"

"Why? You want to go beat her up?" he smiled at her outrage.

"How about an arrow through her nasty heart. Remember, I do have skills."

"How do you know I didn't deserve it?"

"If you were willing to do the whole mate thing with her I seriously doubt you deserved to die."

He stared at her for half a heart beat. Aww screw it. He pulled her into his arms and snuggled her so close they were almost one. She'd sleep in his arms whether he slept or not. He didn't want a night to pass she didn't feel how much she meant to him.

"Go to sleep, Allison. It's been a long couple of days and we've got plenty to do tomorrow."

"Okay, Diego. But just so you know I'm going to dream about hunting her. And I'm going to be very happy about it when I catch her."

Diego laughed. God this woman made him so happy. Diego kissed her one last time and then wrapped his leg around her hips.

"Fine, beautiful. You dream about her. But remember who won okay. If things didn't turn out the way they did, you and I wouldn't be here right now. So as far as I see it, I owe her now.

"You're crazy," she mumbled.

"Right back at you, beautiful. Right back at you."

"Wake up, Romeo. I'm ready to play." She whispered in Diego's ear trying to rouse him from his deep sleep.

She'd crept out of bed as soon as she woke and looked out the window. The clock read 4:30 am and she didn't believe it. It had taken the faint light of the sun just below the horizon to convince her. They'd been asleep for something like sixteen hours.

Now she wanted Diego to wake up too.

She was still hungry. Not as desperate as she'd been in the shower, but sleeping next to his warm, hot body made her dream all kinds of wicked things. Now she wanted to act on them.

But he wasn't budging.

There had to be something she could do to wake him up. That's when the creative light bulb went off. She scrambled up on the bed and pulled the covers back from Diego's body. As she'd discovered when she woke, he was as hard this morning as he'd been when they went to bed.

She wondered what he was dreaming about.

With him so deep in sleep and laid out gloriously naked, she wanted to take some time to savor him. She ran her hand across the ridged expanse of his abdomen, tracing each indentation as she went along until she bumped his erection.

He was so much bigger than she expected and it made her curious to know what he would feel like inside her. Would she stretch enough to accommodate him? She had a hunch she would.

If they were truly fated mates then they were made for each other in every way. Right?

Next, she closed her hand around his cock and admired the weight of it. He was warm too. Rigid and hot. Her mouth watered at the thought, making her even hungrier.

She moved closer and swung her leg over his hips, brushing the tip of him with her eager flesh. She glanced up at him to find him still sleeping.

What the hell? What happened to all his enhanced shifter senses that should have alerted him long ago?

She scooted back into position until she was poised over him. One more little move and she could have him inside her like she craved.

"Dammit, Diego. Wake up."

Suddenly he started laughing. "I was wondering how far you were going to go."

"Seriously? You're awake?"

"Since the moment your body heat rolled away from me."

"Why you..." She rocked backward, feeling his cock begin to part her.

"Whoa." His hands gripped her waist, stilling her. "You don't want to start something you can't finish, beautiful. When I warned you I couldn't stop once we started I wasn't kidding."

"Good. Because like I told you, I've made up my mind." She pushed down a little more and gasped at the sensation of him beginning to fill her.

"Allison. Please. Baby. I'm holding onto my control by a thread."

He wasn't lying. She could see his body begin to tremble as he tried to stop himself.

"Let go and hold onto me," she said. "No, I don't know exactly what I'm doing, but I can't stop feeling like this is right. We're right."

"You'll become a shifter."

"And we'll cross that bridge when we come to it. Together right?" She looked at him, pleading with him to accept her as she was. A human woman unsure of anything except how much she wanted him.

"I can't believe I found you," he whispered, his tone almost guttural. "You're mine."

"And you're mine." Except right now he was slowly killing her by holding back.

"Please, Diego. I want this."

Diego clenched his jaw and released her hips, leaving the final decision to move forward or not completely up to her.

"If you want me, Allison. Then take me."

She almost cried at the beautiful gesture he'd just made. Her big, beautiful shifter would never do anything to her she would regret. She loved that about him.

With his gaze locked onto hers she bit her bottom lip and pushed him all the way in. She tried to take a breath and couldn't. He was hot and large, spreading her open.

"So fucking beautiful," he groaned.

He was right about that. The two of them joined together made her want to weep with amazement. Something inside her shifted and her heart cracked wide.

It was joy. A happiness so pure she thought it might break her.

He grabbed her hips and began to guide her movements. "Nice and easy. Let your body adjust."

Adjust hell, she was going to explode before they even got started. She rocked her hips and took back the control, driving him deeper than before.

She looked down to see where they were joined and gasped. Her sexy shifter was inside her and it was glorious. Her eyes skimmed his abs and chest again before settling on his gaze.

She licked her lips. "You still hungry?"

"Hell yes, beautiful."

That's all it took for her to move. She rocked back and forth a few times before she caught the rhythm and then it was on. Her deep thoughts of mating melded into the need so deep in her gut she didn't know how to get it out.

Diego knifed forward and wrapped her in his strong arms as they moved in tandem. She couldn't believe how safe she felt with him. Feeling lucky, Allison peppered kisses along his jaw and neck as he helped her increase her speed. The ache inside her was already beginning to build. Soon it would be unbearable.

"You're so damned perfect, Allison. In every way. This is where I truly belong. Inside my mate."

They were rocking frantically now, making her breasts sway. She reached down and squeezed the tips watching his eyes turn gold as she did.

"Do that again," he ordered, his eyes growing brighter.

With a half smile and hooded eyes, she pinched her nipples and pulled.

"I think I'm going to stay like this forever," he panted.

She clung to his shoulders. Their mating season might be officially over, but her frenzy wasn't. Her body burned where he pushed inside her, igniting delicious friction each time.

Sweat slicked their skin as he gripped her harder and drove into her as fast as she pushed down.

Frantic.

Out of control.

Wet.

Tight.

Hard.

She couldn't think as every sensation exploded together. She screamed as Diego came inside her, his ferocious growl echoing her shouts.

His arms wrapped around her shoulders and held them tight together as he continued to pulse inside her.

"Diego," she cried as little aftershocks went off again and again. The tears she'd never once shed, slid down her face as the joy inside her swelled. Her heart was warm and open. So open.

His thrusts slowed and finally stopped. She dropped her head on his shoulder and reveled in his warmth. It didn't matter. Their differences were stupid.

"I've been such an idiot," she said, her breath still heavy.

"What on earth are you talking about?" He pulled back just enough to force her to raise her head.

"How many years did I waste believing in terrible things?" She squeezed her eyes closed trying to forget.

"You can't think like that. Fate works the way it's supposed to. I didn't believe it either until you showed up. If we weren't the people we are with the experiences we've had, we wouldn't be here right now."

She opened her eyes. "You really believe that?"

He nodded. "I do now. And I've got a hot mate to prove it. And she's a she wolf in the sheets."

Allison smiled. You're crazy. I don't know what you did to me, but that was all you."

He nuzzled her hair. "I beg to differ, mate. Shall I show you what I mean?"

"Well..." she looked up at him through her lashes. "I am still hungry."

Diego rolled them in the sheets, keeping them joined together. "Ooh look who's the animal now. We've created a monster."

"Romeo can't handle it after all?" She smiled at how good he made her feel. Teasing him was so much fun.

He swooped down and nibbled on her jaw. "Oh it's on now, beautiful. Prepare yourself for the onslaught of pleasure."

Allison grinned, holding onto his warmth. Life thus far had taken her down some dark and twisted turns, but they were all worth it to end up here...

With the mate of her dreams.

———— ❖ ————

Thank you so much for reading!

WANT to know what happens next? You can in FERAL right now!

MATING SEASON MAY BE OVER, **but Brody Fox is still going insane.** He's angry, resentful and probably dangerous. And he can't stop dreaming about the brown-eyed girl he wants to bite. Please look for **FERAL**, now available.

Join Eliza's VIP newsletter at elizagayle.com/newsletter and be the first to be notified of new releases, sales and contests.

Continue reading for a bonus chapter from FERAL, the next book in the Devils Point Wolves series and the full booklist from Eliza Gayle.

114

SNEAK PEEK FROM FERAL

FERAL

By Eliza Gayle
Copyright 2015
All Rights Reserved

Book Description:

All it takes is one time...

Prue Davis is desperate. Her boss has gone nuts trying to show everyone his 'mangina', her research has been confiscated and her only hope of salvaging her career is to return to Devils Point Island and find out why so many wild wolves are drawn to one small island. She thinks she's prepared, but no one is ever ready to find out their new lover is a werewolf.

Mating Season is over, but Brody Fox is still going insane. He's angry, resentful and probably dangerous. And he can't stop dreaming about the brown-eyed girl he wants to bite. Now he's ready to do or say anything to find the mate he lost. But if one more person calls him feral...

Chapter One

Brody stared out at the rocky beach from the inside of his tiny eight by eight cell unsure if he'd last another day in this hell hole. As far as holding cells went, this one wasn't so bad. The room was clean and he had a comfortable bed with plenty to eat.

None of which did a damn bit of good when the wolf inside him stirred constantly. If this is what it felt like to live with multiple personalities then those afflicted had his heartfelt sympathy because this shit sucked, keeping him on edge day and night.

The security detail assigned to watch over him kept calling him feral and he was sick and tired of hearing that too.

Several of the pack assured him he'd only be held here until they were certain he wasn't a danger to anyone else. But he knew better. In the midst of his frenzy he'd bitten an innocent girl, the mate to one of the pack leaders as it turned out. She survived, but that situation did not bode well for him and he knew it.

Not that he blamed them.

He spent his whole life hating and hunting down shapeshifters without ever understanding anything about them. Shifters called the hunters fanatics where Brody simply called them family.

Now, forced to walk in their skin it was easy to see just how narrow-minded he had been. Is that the way it always went? Hindsight and all that bullshit.

A growl formed deep in his throat. With the sun hidden behind the dark grey clouds, the outside seemed to match his inside as a storm continued to brew.

In the midst of his confusion after being accidentally bitten, the scent of a mate had given him hope and lured him to Devil's Point Island.

The disappearance of that scent had created a monster. One that refused to settle down no matter how hard he tried.

According to the pack living here on the island, his frenzy should have ended with mating season. The one time of year when all wolves go a little crazy with the need to find and bond with a mate. Only it didn't.

Weeks had passed and nothing changed. He still wanted to tear down the walls of his cell brick by brick and go on a hunt. Except he had no clue where to start.

The beautiful brown-haired girl he'd found on the beach had disappeared just as she appeared—without a trace.

After first scenting her in wolf form, he'd followed her scent for miles before finally coming upon her sitting on the beach in front of a campfire roasting marshmallows and laughing with her friends.

Night had fallen and the golden glow of the burning logs cast an ethereal aura around her. Instead of shifting and approaching her, he'd been a dumb ass and chosen to sit on his haunches and watch her from afar.

After traveling so long to catch her and not understanding the irresistible draw, he simply wanted to savor the moment.

He couldn't see the color of her eyes and had no idea what her name was, but in the soft light with the cool breeze blowing through his fur, none of that mattered.

Listening to her laugh with her scent wrapping around him calmed the chaos raging inside him. For the first time in weeks he'd felt a semblance of peace. Something even his human life never gave him.

Of course he'd been an idiot and waited too long. By the time he was ready to talk to her she'd disappeared into her tent and he didn't want to scare her by stalking her in her sleep.

Instead, he resigned himself to let them both get some rest before he approached her. He took cover in the tree line for the night and laid his body down in a soft spot of grass and fell asleep almost before his chin hit the ground.

When he woke she was gone. Somehow he'd slept through her departure and no amount of searching the island and surrounding areas had turned up even a trace of her.

He'd lost his *mate.*

His human side still balked at the idea of a fated mate. His sister, Allison, had been led down that path not long ago and now seemed somewhat settled with her new mate Diego. She visited him everyday and he believed she might be happy if not for the worry lines that creased her forehead every time she saw him.

Brody pulled his gaze back from the beach and dropped to the floor and began doing push ups. Since he couldn't run free, he was forced to do calisthenics to ease some of the energy constantly overloading his system.

It didn't exactly work. But it made him almost civil so he continued to do it everyday.

Like every other day the number of reps flew by, sweat coated his body and his brain temporarily focused on the task at hand.

He wasn't thinking about anything beyond the determination to keep going so the new scent from the open window slammed into him unexpectedly.

Brody dropped and rolled, his hands ripping at the pants that confined his shift.

It couldn't be.

Before he registered what was happening claws tore at his zipper as he began to change and he barely got the denim off his legs before the bones popped and fur sprouted across his body.

He jumped on the window and inhaled deep, sticking his snout through the bars. It was there. The unmistakable scent of the woman never far from his mind.

No way.

The wolf began clawing at the walls below the window despite the fact the concrete construction gave him absolutely no way out.

He didn't care. All that mattered was getting to the woman he needed more than anything else. He scratched and scraped until his forearms ached and his claws were worn down to the quick.

"Brody, what the hell are you doing?"

The wolf jerked at the sound of his sister's voice behind him, giving his human half a chance to regain control. As quickly as he shifted to wolf, he changed back.

"Holy shit." Allison jerked away from him and turned her back. "Give a girl some warning. I do not need to see your junk—Ever!"

He looked down at his nudity and almost smiled. Any other time he would have teased her mercilessly about being so squeamish. Not today. Not when the answer to his prayers stood right in front of him.

"Allison, you've got to get me out of here." He grabbed his pants and shoved his legs in them, barely taking the two seconds to fasten the zipper and button.

"You know I can't do that." She sighed. "How many times are we going to go over this? It's not safe. "

"For who?" he growled. "Me? You?"

"The whole pack, Brody. This isn't just about you and me anymore. There's a lot more at stake."

He rolled his eyes and groaned. "I can't believe how easily you accepted the whole pack mentality. What happened to bucking the system? Being an individual? Not being a sheep?"

"Because we're not human anymore," she hissed. "Wolves need the pack."

"So you've said."

"I'm not the only one," she retorted. "Don't discount what Diego and his brothers have to say. They've dealt with ferals before."

He cringed at the word. The fact even his sister called him that did not give him much of a chance. But he had to try.

"Have they ever saved a feral? It would seem our captors don't say much about that."

"We aren't captives."

He looked around his small room. "Really? I know I can't go anywhere. Are you so sure you can? What if you wanted to leave the island?"

"Don't be ridiculous. I chose this life. I chose Diego and I'm happier for it. Can't you understand that? We just need to stick together. All of us. The pack."

He stepped forward and leaned against the plexiglass that separated them. "If that's true then how am I supposed to be getting better being isolated in here? It's impossible to acclimate in isolation."

She shook her head. "I'm not letting you out. Not until Diego says it's safe."

Brody banged his hand on the clear divider. "Don't be like this, Sis. I'm not trying to get free so I can go on some insane killing spree. Being locked up is the problem. I just want..." He stopped, unable to say the words even to his sister.

"You want what?" Suspicion rose in her voice.

He considered his next words carefully. He didn't like having to manipulate her, but he was desperate. No way in hell he'd lose the woman on the beach twice.

"There's a woman. I can smell her."

Allison crunched up her face. "Eww, seriously? I don't want to hear this."

"Oh for fuck's sake. I am not talking about sex. She is far more important than that. It's the mate bond." He swallowed down the distaste of his lies. But he had to do something...

"We connected during mating season before I understood what was happening. She was here on vacation, but by the time I realized the true nature of what she was to me she'd left the island."

Allison's stance and features were softening as he spoke. The curse of someone in love is that they want everyone around them to be in love too. It made his sister easy prey.

"I saw her on the beach this morning. She's returned and I think she's pregnant with my baby."

Her hand flew to her mouth. "How can you be so sure?"

He tapped his nose. "Heightened senses, baby. This thing tells me all kinds of stuff now."

She nodded, obviously agreeing with him.

"So you see? You have to help me get out of here so I can find her. I can't let my pregnant mate suffer."

Suddenly the sound of clapping filled his small cell and Creed, one of the men keeping any eye on him, walked out of the shadows.

"Wow. That was quite a performance. That's some serious balls you've got there to feed that bullshit to your sister though."

Allison's face hardened and her eyes narrowed. "Is that what you were doing? Lying to me to get what you wanted?"

When he didn't immediately answer she stomped her foot and exited the room without another word.

"Thanks, bro," Brody muttered.

Creed smiled back at him. "I don't think she was going to let you out anyway. Diego would have given her hell and probably tried to lock her up again."

"What do you mean again?"

He shrugged. "They didn't exactly meet under the best of circumstances. Before he figured out what to do with her he had to detain her somehow."

Brody shook his head. "Let me guess. It didn't work."

"Nope," Creed paused. "I heard she got herself free in less than ten minutes."

"That's my sister. The escape artist."

"Too bad you didn't get that trait. Maybe you wouldn't be making up strange stories to get loose."

"It wasn't all lies," Brody said. "I did sort of meet a woman during mating season."

"And? Don't leave a brother hanging. Mating season is a kick ass time for us unattached wolves. For some it means finding the elusive true mate. As for the rest of us, we just want to screw every available woman who will have us. "

Brody had to fight the urge to lash out at Creed. As much as he respected the man for his loyalty to the pack and the respect he gave him, he didn't like his mystery woman being lumped in with the conquests he and Sawyer bragged about.

"It wasn't like that. There was—I don't know—something about her scent that made me feel different."

"No shit. Are you serious?"

Brody lifted his shoulders. "Like I said. No big deal."

"Uh huh. Did her scent make you desperate to get close to her? Or did you feel unusually settled when you were around her?"

Yes. It was exactly like that, but he didn't like the direction Creed was headed. He didn't want to talk about their mating crap anymore.

"I wouldn't know. Before I could talk to her I got a text from Allison that she was on the island looking for me. I took cover and by the time I made it back to the beach, the woman was gone."

The other man nodded. "I knew you were bullshitting Allison. She is going to kick your ass."

"Probably. If I ever get out of here that is. Not a whole lot she can do with me in here and her out there." He was really fighting the need to snarl at Creed by this point. The scent of the woman on the beach was making the damned wolf insane, beating at his brain.

"Was anything you said real? Or are you bullshitting me too? I've got a much better nose for lies than your newbie sister."

"I caught her scent again." His words were clipped as the aggression in him rose.

"And you need to get out there, don't you? The wolf is riding your ass to do something and do something quick."

He nodded, gritting his teeth. "How do you know? You aren't mated. Not that I'm putting a lot of stock in that nonsense."

Creed reached into his pocket and pulled out his keys. "That's a story for another day." He slid the metal into the cell lock and opened the door.

"Don't make me regret this. If you pull something stupid I will put you down and then I'm going to be really pissed."

Brody failed to see how his logic worked, but he didn't care. The only thing standing between him and freedom was this one shifter. And he was willing to tell him anything he wanted to hear if it meant he got what he wanted.

"You won't regret it. Unless you keep toying with me. Then we'll both have regrets."

READ MORE NOW

ALSO BY ELIZA GAYLE

The Dragon Lore Trilogy:

THE CURSE OF THE DRAGON

THE SOUL OF THE DRAGON

THE FIRE OF THE DRAGON

Southern Shifters Series:

SHIFTER MARKED

MATE NIGHT

ALPHA KNOWS BEST

BAD KITTY

BE WERE

SHIFTIN' DIRTY

BEAR NAKED TRUTH

ALPHA BEAST

ONE CRAZY WOLF

Enigma Shifters Fated Mates:

DRAGON MATED

WOLF BAITED

BEARLY DATED

WOLF TEMPTED

Devils Point Wolves:

WILD

WICKED

WANTED

FERAL

FIERCE

FURY

Single titles:

VAMPIRE AWAKENING

WITCH AND WERE

WRITING AS E.M. GAYLE
CONTEMPORARY ROMANCE

Mafia Mayhem Duet Series:

MERCILESS SINNER

SINNER TAKES ALL

WICKED BEAST

WILLING BEAUTY

BROKEN SAINT

FALLEN ANGEL

Outlaw Justice Series:

SAVAGE PROTECTOR

RECKLESS PAWN

RUTHLESS REDEMPTION

Outlaw Justice: Sins of Wrath MC:

CRUEL SAVIOR

SCORCHED KING

VICIOUS DEFENDER

Purgatory Masters Series:

TUCKER'S FALL

LEVI'S ULTIMATUM

MASON'S RULE

GABE'S OBSESSION

GABE'S RECKONING

Purgatory Club:

ROPED

WATCH ME

TEASED

BURN

BOTTOMS UP

HOLD ME CLOSE

Pleasure Playground Series:

PLAY WITH ME

POWER PLAY

Single Title:

TAMING BEAUTY

WICKED CHRISTMAS EVE